W9-AYP-678

Horseshoes
#3
Cross-Country
GALLOP

**Written by Patricia Leitch**

HarperCollins*Publishers*

*This series is for Meg*

First published in Great Britain by Lions, an imprint of HarperCollins Publishers, in 1993.

**CROSS-COUNTRY GALLOP**
 Printed in the United States of America.
For information address HarperCollins Children's Books, a division of HarperCollins Publishers, 10 East 53rd Street, New York, NY 10022.

Library of Congress Cataloging-in-Publication Data
Leitch, Patricia.
Cross-country gallop / written by Patricia Leitch.
p. cm. — (Horseshoes ; #3)
Summary: When ten-year-olds Sally and Thalia decide to compete in the horse show as a pair, they place severe strains on their nerves and on their friendship.
ISBN 0-06-440636-9 (pbk.) — ISBN 0-06-027287-2 (lib. bdg.)
[1. Horses—Fiction. 2. Horse shows—Fiction. 3. Friendship—Fiction.] I. Title. II. Series: Leitch, Patricia. Horseshoes ; #3.
PZ7.L5372Cr 1996 96-4902
[Fic]—dc20 CIP
AC

Typography by Darcy Soper
1 2 3 4 5 6 7 8 9 10
❖
First Edition

*Also by Patricia Leitch*

*Horseshoes #1*
*THE PERFECT HORSE*

*Horseshoes #2*
*JUMPING LESSONS*

*Horseshoes #4*
*PONY CLUB RIDER*

Horseshoes
#3
Cross-Country
GALLOP

# *Chapter One*

Sally Lorimer was ten years old. She was not tall, not small; not fat, not skinny. She had thick brown bangs and hair that fell straight to her shoulders, wide-set blue eyes, and a quirky mouth that turned up at the corners. Sprawled out on the long grass that grew like a meadow around the ruined summerhouse, she stared out at the glint and glimmer of the summer sea. Behind her was the overgrown garden that reached to the high stone tower of Kestrel Manor—a huge stone house, built on its own peninsula of land, where Sally and her family lived.

Stretched out at Sally's side lay Thalia ("Rhymes-with-dahlia-which-is-a-flower-like-a-chrysanthemum") Nesbit. Thalia, too, was ten years old. She was long and lean with a fizzing sunburst of corn-colored hair. Thalia's parents were divorced, and she lived with her narg—*gran* spelled backward—in a cottage by the shore, close to Kestrel Manor.

"She did mean it, didn't she?" Sally demanded, turning her head so that she could see the horses' field with its wide-spreading chestnut tree and its new fencing. She had to sit up to see the horses—Tarquin, the sleek roan who belonged to Thalia, and—grazing close beside him—Willow, her own dapple-gray with a silver mane and tail.

"Yes, she meant it," said Thalia, propping herself up on one elbow and grinning with delight at sea, sun, and grazing horses. "Martine said she was very pleased with our progress, that we had both improved beyond belief. Though you could hardly hear her for that man shouting at the boy. But that is what she said."

" 'Improved beyond belief.' " Sally repeated the words like a charm. Magic words, as magic as the tiny crystal unicorn she had found one day while standing at the edge of the sea. She had crouched down to discover what it was that was glinting there under the water. A wave had carried the unicorn into the palm of her hand, as if the sea had given it to her.

Sally searched in the pocket of her jodhpurs

and set the unicorn in the center of her hand. Rainbow light sparkled from it.

"Did it all happen because of the unicorn?" Sally wondered. "Because it found me? Because it was waiting for me?"

She shut her eyes and tried to remember back to the beginning, six long months ago, when the Lorimers had gone for a picnic at Fintry Bay.

There were five human Lorimers. Mr. Lorimer was a librarian. Mrs. Lorimer painted landscapes in flowing watercolors and was busy-about-the-house only when there was absolutely nothing else worth doing. Ben Lorimer was fifteen and the oldest child. He was tall, with a shock of black hair like his father's, and always had his nose in a book. Sally fitted in next, and then there was Jamie, the youngest Lorimer, at four.

The day of the picnic was the day Sally had found the unicorn. And it was the day they had driven past Kestrel Manor, which was still empty and deserted. Mr. Lorimer had stopped the car at the foot of Kestrel Manor's drive to let them dream for a minute about what it would be like if only they had enough money to buy the house and live there.

"Then," thought Sally, "we were an ordinary family living in a dull, ordinary house, suffocated by car fumes and noise. And me, dragging up and down the lane at Miss Meek's riding school, just dying because I didn't have a horse of my own." But then everything changed.

The very next Friday *the* letter had arrived for Mr. Lorimer. A great-uncle whom Mr. Lorimer had hardly known had died in Australia, leaving Mr. Lorimer what the lawyers called "a considerable sum of money." In an almost unimaginable, magical happening, they had bought Kestrel Manor and now were living there. Thalia was Sally's friend and kept Tarquin with Willow.

"Willow, my own horse. . . ." Sally opened her eyes to gaze lovingly at the dapple-gray horse whisking flies away with sweeps of her long, silver tail.

Until Sally had found Willow, her riding had been a bit of a mess. There had been her disastrous runaway ride on Tarquin, leaving Sally afraid to gallop. But then she had found Willow and everything had changed. And now, after a course of jumping lessons, Sally's jumping had improved so much that Martine Dawes, their instructor at Mr. Frazer's elegant riding school, had said, and Sally repeated the words yet again, that she had " 'improved beyond belief.' "

"Do you think she said that because she saw us jumping the wall with Nick Ross?" she asked Thalia.

"Thirty-foot spread," exaggerated Thalia. "At least twenty feet high."

Yesterday they had been riding in a pageant. Sally and Thalia had jumped into a walled garden, riding behind Nick Ross on his famous show-jumper Rose of Sharon.

"Forty feet?" suggested Sally, and she rolled out on the warm grass, reliving the moment when Willow had soared over the wall and she had sat, securely balanced, loving every minute of it.

"Perfect!" said Thalia. "Absolutely perfect. And now the Tarent Horse Show on Saturday. Show jumping and pairs cross-country."

At Thalia's words Sally felt her stomach tighten nervously. Saturday would be the first time she had jumped in a competition. What if she fell off? What if she made a fool of Willow? Perhaps she should have stayed at Miss Meek's riding school; perhaps all she was fit for was to ride Miss Meek's shabby ponies up and down the lane.

"Don't be so stupid," Sally told herself. "You have left all that behind you."

But she hadn't. There was still something, something she had pushed to the back of her mind, something she couldn't allow herself to think about.

Suddenly Willow buckled at the knees and rolled over to rub and scratch herself on the ground. Three times she pushed herself from side to side, her shoes flashing white fire, before she struggled upright, stretched out her neck, and, balancing herself on propped legs, shook herself violently.

And in that instant Sally knew. She couldn't keep herself from remembering. That was the way Miss Meek's horses had rolled after their hard day's work in the riding school. Sally had loved all the horses in the riding school, but especially a black horse called Clover. She had been the one that Sally had always ridden; the horse that might have been grazing in the field with Tarquin. But Sally had told her father that she did not want Clover, did not want him to buy a riding-school pony for her. In her mind's eye Sally saw Clover standing in her fenced-in strip of field, trying to nibble at the overgrazed grass, the saddle mark still imprinted on her back.

And I turned and left her, Sally thought, and because the memory hurt so much, she had to talk to Thalia about it.

"Remember I told you about Miss Meek's riding school? In Matwood, where I used to ride? Remember Clover? How I told Dad I didn't want her?"

"Well, you didn't," said Thalia. "She didn't sound to me as if she would have been much use."

"But maybe now that I've improved a bit, perhaps . . ."

"You wouldn't have improved if you hadn't been riding Willow. If you had let your dad buy Clover, you'd never have found Willow. True?"

"I suppose so . . ."

*"True,"* said Thalia. "So don't start. Now, where are we going to practice for the cross-country? We haven't much time to build a course, but we could build some jumps in the field so we can practice jumping together. Really we only have four days, because I've got to go to the dentist on Wednesday."

"Right," agreed Sally, realizing suddenly that it was only five days until the Tarent Horse Show.

"The obstacles won't be very big. What the judges want to see is us keeping together between the jumps and taking off and landing at exactly the same time. Whee!" Thalia's arm traced a wide arc against sea and sky, making Sally wonder just what size the obstacles would really be. As she imagined massed tree trunks, brush jumps, walls, and ditches, the memory of Clover slipped to the back of her mind again, almost forgotten.

"So you *must* wake Willow up, let her gallop on. She must keep up with Tarquin."

"And you," said Sally, "will have to control Tarquin. Not let him race out of control."

"Tarquin is never out of control. . . ."

"Sally! Sally!" called Ben. "Where are you?"

Sally jumped to her feet, waving her arms above her head.

"Here," she yelled. "By the summerhouse."

Ben came racing toward them, first over the roughly cut grass they called the lawn and then through the long grass.

Misty, the Lorimers' gray-and-white bearded collie, leaped at Ben's side, barking hysterically, her long coat flying out about her like a Chinese dragon's. Behind them both, Meg, the Lorimers' other Beardie, panted to keep up. Meg was black and white. She was twelve years old, which Mrs. Lorimer called a good age but really meant that she was getting old, more ready to lie on the ground and bark at a noise than go bustling and bounding to discover what was happening.

Sally could see Ben's mouth opening and closing, but she couldn't hear what he was saying because of Misty's noise.

"Shut up!" Sally yelled. "Button it, Misty!"

"These Beardies," exclaimed Ben, reaching Sally. "It's the phone for you. Something about practicing for the cross-country at the show."

Thalia sprang to her feet. Grabbing Sally's hand, she raced her toward the house.

"Cross-country," she yelled. "A practice for the cross-country. That is just what we need."

## *Chapter Two*

They ran through the kitchen, narrowly missing Sally's mother, and on into the hall. Sally picked up the receiver, but her breathless "Hello" was met with a humming silence.

"There's no one there," she said.

"There must be," declared Thalia. Grabbing the phone from Sally, she yelled, "Hello! Hello! Hello!"

"Unfortunately," said Mr. Lorimer, "telephones do not respond to shouting. If they've hung up, you've had it."

He took the receiver from Thalia, tried one "Hello" of his own, and hung up.

"She sounded young," said Ben, coming into the kitchen. "About Sally's age."

"Didn't she say who she was?" cried Thalia.

"Uh-uh," said Ben, shaking his head. "Only something about the Pony Club."

"The Pony Club!" exclaimed Thalia. "Oh, you should have told them to hold on."

"I did," said Ben, scowling at Thalia. "How

was I to know you two would be at the back of beyond?"

"Whoever it was, I'm sure they'll call back," soothed Mrs. Lorimer.

"I'd have thought you were a founding member of the Pony Club," Mr. Lorimer said to Thalia.

"Well, no," said Thalia. "Actually no, because before you came to Kestrel Manor I didn't want anyone to find out where I was keeping Tarquin. Some nosy Pony Club mom telling the police that I was keeping him here without permission and Tarquin would've had to live in Narg's toolshed. Not much room."

"While you were in prison for trespassing?" suggested Ben.

"But of course," agreed Thalia. "And I want you to know I am humble and grateful for all I receive. So are Narg's spades and forks and clippers and shears and flowerpots, for not having to share their home with a horse."

"Okay, okay," said Mr. Lorimer. "Grateful you may be, but humble you are not, and thank goodness for that."

Mrs. Lorimer handed around chips and

lemonade. Before they had finished drinking, the phone rang again. Sally reached it first.

"Could I speak to Sally Lorimer?"

"That's me," said Sally.

"Oh, good. I'm Verity Blair, and Mom asked me to phone. We're having a practice for the cross-country events at the Tarent show. Martine Dawes told us that you had entered, so would you like to come?"

"Me too," breathed Thalia.

"When is it?" asked Sally, a mixture of excitement and nerves tingling her spine.

"Tomorrow. Eleven o'clock."

"Can I come too?" Thalia demanded, speaking into the phone.

"Are you the other girl who jumped the wall with Nick Ross?"

"Yes, on Tarquin."

"Then you're invited. Mom just didn't know where to find you. Here's Mom to speak to Sally's mother. See you tomorrow. Bye."

"That was Mrs. Blair," said Mrs. Lorimer when she had finished speaking on the phone.

"Then it is the Pony Club. Mrs. Blair organizes the Pony Club."

"We're all invited to go to their house tomorrow. Eleven o'clock. You two are to ride and we are to be your support group. Apparently they have a cross-country course on their grounds, which sounds very grand to me."

"And we have to jump it?" demanded Sally.

"Well, it sounded like it to me."

"Of course you have to jump," exclaimed Thalia in disgust. "You're jumping with me in five days, aren't you? I've told you, Willow will love it as long as you don't try to hold her back. Just make her keep up with me!"

Before Sally had time to answer back, the phone rang again.

"Martine Dawes," said Mr. Lorimer after he had answered it. "She's taking a horse over to Ashdale—that's the Blairs' house—for the practice tomorrow. A man is hiring a horse for the day for his son to ride. There will be room in the trailer for your two. She'll pick you up at ten. And she says although it won't be superfancy, you had better look respectable."

"Well, of all the nerve," said Mrs. Lorimer. "Sally always does."

"Don't worry, Mrs. Lorimer," said Thalia.

"She means me. Even when Narg does her very best, I still look sort of ratty. Can't help it. It's my nature. Better start now—clean tack, wash hair, and up at dawn to groom."

They were ready before ten the next morning, standing in the stable yard waiting for the sound of a horse trailer turning up Kestrel Manor's drive. Willow and Tarquin looked over the half-doors of their stalls, their coats gleaming, hoofs oiled, and halters over their bridles.

"I expect we'll arrive just after you," said Mrs. Lorimer, who was waiting to see them off. "I have to pick up Narg. We're bringing a picnic."

"The last thing I could possibly do is eat," thought Sally, but she said nothing, knowing that her mother would fuss.

"Here she is," shouted Thalia. They all heard the heavy rumble of a horse trailer trundling up the drive.

They led their horses out into the yard. Tarquin's head was held high on his giraffe's neck, his nostrils wide, his ears sharp as he pranced at Thalia's side. Willow stood with her front hoofs neatly together, her dark eyes bright, waiting calmly to see what was going to happen next.

Martine was driving, and a boy who looked about ten or eleven was sitting next to her. He had straight blond hair that fell over his dark eyes. His shoulders were hunched forward, and even when Martine jumped down from the cab he didn't look up, just sat looking down at his hands.

"Hi! Great day. Glad you're on time. Let's get them on board. Have they been in a horse trailer before?"

"Don't know," chorused Sally and Thalia.

"We'll soon find out," said Martine, lowering the ramp.

There was a chestnut horse tied at the far end of the trailer, held in place by a wooden bar.

"Dragonfly. For Simon to ride. Definitely, but definitely, *not* the horse I would have chosen for Simon to ride. Once Mr. Knowles starts shouting, though, he usually gets what he wants. Now, lead Willow in first. Walk straight in. Don't let her stop."

Sally gulped. Then, leading Willow by her halter, she walked smartly up the ramp into the vast darkness of the trailer. Willow's ears flickered. She whinnied, a small questioning sound.

"It's all right," whispered Sally. "There's a good girl. On we go."

Willow's hoofs tip-tapped on the hollow-sounding ramp as she followed Sally obediently into the trailer.

"What a good horse," praised Martine, taking the halter rope from Sally and tying Willow up with a quick-release knot. "Wish they were all like her." Sally grinned with pride.

"Now Tarquin."

Thalia rushed Tarquin at the ramp.

"Steady," Martine warned. "Take it easy."

As they reached the ramp, Tarquin reared up. He tossed his head, neighing wildly, making Mrs. Lorimer back off to a safe distance. When he felt the wood under his front hoofs, he spun around and, dragging Thalia, tried to canter off.

Martine sprang to grab Tarquin's bridle, but Thalia was faster. Catching Tarquin's bit-ring, she pulled his head around.

"Idiot," she told him. "Behave yourself. Get into the trailer."

And almost before Tarquin realized what was

happening, Thalia was running him toward the ramp. At the exact moment when he was about to rear again, Thalia slapped the halter rope hard on his neck and roared at him to stop messing around. With a huge leap Tarquin stormed into the trailer. By the time Martine reached Thalia, she was praising her horse, feeding him peppermints and telling him what a brave boy he was.

Martine regarded Thalia with raised eyebrows.

"Perhaps if you had taken things easier from the beginning?" she suggested.

"That wouldn't have worked," Thalia assured her. "You've got to be quick with Tarquin. He's not Willow."

"Well," said Martine, "your timing was just right."

The horse trailer rattled over the country roads to Ashdale. Martine drove with easy confidence. The boy whom Martine had introduced as Simon Knowles was squashed against the cab window while Sally balanced on Thalia's knee. Behind Thalia's head was a small window into the back of the trailer. Peering through it, Sally could just make out the dim shapes of the horses, the glint of the white of an eye, the arch of a neck, and dust motes dazzling in a beam of light that sprayed over Willow's dappled quarters.

Sally swallowed hard. In less than an hour she would be galloping Willow at cross-country jumps. Suddenly her old fear gripped her—the fear of being thrown off Tarquin into the rusty nails of the jetty. She couldn't help thinking of all the dreadful times she had been left behind when Willow jumped, always getting thrown over Willow's head when she landed.

" 'Improved beyond belief.' " Sally repeated Martine's praise to encourage herself. "If only that man hadn't been shouting so much, I could have heard her better. . . ." Sally stopped short in mid-thought, for of course Simon Knowles, the boy sitting next to them in the cab, was the same boy. Vaguely Sally remembered that the man had been telling the boy that he must have a horse to ride on Monday.

And the horse he is to ride is Dragonfly, from Mr. Frazer's stables!

Sally twisted her head around so she could get a better look at Simon. Totally ignoring Thalia's incessant chatter, he was staring determinedly out the cab window.

"How long have you been in the Pony Club?" Sally asked him.

Simon twitched away from her words, turned his shoulder against her, and went on staring at the passing scenery.

"Here we are," announced Martine as she drove past a high beech hedge and wrought-iron gates, and turned down a rutted lane that took them into the grounds of Ashdale. They went through a field gate to where several trailers were already parked and children were riding around.

"Everybody out," said Martine, jumping down from the cab.

Sally and Thalia scooted over to the driver's seat and leaped out. Simon sat still, ignoring them.

The ramp of the horse trailer was lowered. Martine untied Tarquin, who surged out of the trailer. Willow whinnied a welcome to Sally and stepped carefully down the ramp. Martine led out the prancing chestnut horse.

"Where's Simon?" she asked.

"Still in the cab," said Thalia.

"Tell him to come and take Dragonfly," Martine said, then hesitated. "No, don't bother. Here comes Mr. Ronald Knowles in person. Cover up your ear holes!"

"Simon! Simon!" roared a man's voice. "Come on. Wake up. *Now!* At once. *Now!* Get out of that trailer *now*! I'm not hiring that horse to have you sitting sleeping all day. Out, I tell you. *Out!*"

Mr. Knowles came striding toward the horse trailer. To Sally he looked like a furious scarecrow. His bony wrists stuck out of his tweed jacket, and his head—with its bushy crop of short black hair—burst out of his polo-necked sweater. All his jangling energy was aimed at Simon.

Sally swallowed hard, glad that Mr. Knowles was not her father.

Simon opened the cab door and slid to the ground without looking at his father.

"I do not know," said Martine aloud, to herself, "why he won't leave Simon alone. Poor kid, having to cope with him as well as everything else."

## *Chapter Three*

"Hello. I'm Verity Blair," said a dark-haired girl with glasses and rosy cheeks, riding up to Sally on a thick-set bay. "I called you. We're all very glad you could come. Mom's always desperate to find new members for the Pony Club. We're such a measly small branch."

"Oh," said Sally, wondering if Verity's mother would still be glad to see her if she fell off Willow. Sally could see what looked like the first two jumps of the cross-country course—two telephone poles and then a brush jump.

Sally's heart sank. Really she hadn't done any cross-country jumping. The red-and-white poles in the paddock of Mr. Frazer's riding school suddenly seemed quite safe compared to galloping over rough ground where rabbit burrows or loose stones might bring Willow to her knees. Just as her imagination was taking over, transforming the small Pony Club–size obstacles into insurmountable barriers, Sally remembered the unicorn lying in her pocket. She took it out and it sparkled in the palm of her hand.

"I'm Thalia Nesbit," announced Thalia. "You said I was supposed to come too."

"Oh, yes. Mom knew you lived somewhere around here, but she could never find out where. We called you the Vanishing Rider."

"Well, here I am now. Can we see the jumps?" said Thalia, quickly changing the subject.

"Over this way," said Verity, turning her horse and leading the way out of the field. They rode along a lane and through an open gate to a stretch of rough country.

"Whee!" enthused Thalia. "Super!" Standing up in her stirrups, she gazed around at a course of about fifteen obstacles.

First there were the two jumps that Sally had seen from the field; then the course followed a track through bracken. Then it ran down a slope that seemed to Sally as steep as a playground slide, and on over a stream and a wall, finishing with a series of metal drums.

"Don't worry," said Verity, seeing Sally's

stricken expression. "That's the full course. We'll only be jumping a few of them. Mom is very cautious."

"But I want to jump them all!" exclaimed Thalia. "Could I have a try now?"

"No, you could not. I'm not even allowed to ride around it unless it's official."

"But no one would know," said Thalia. To Sally's horror she began to gather in her reins, ready to ride over the obstacles.

"Oh, yes they would," said Verity. "Here they come." But she was smiling, her eyes dancing at Thalia's daring.

Thalia looked back over her shoulder. She saw nine horses and riders, led on foot by Mrs. Blair, coming out of the lane. Behind them were about twenty parents and friends, including Sally's mother and Thalia's narg.

"Gosh," said Thalia. "Good thing I didn't. Narg would have splattered me."

"But you would have gone around, wouldn't you?" asked Verity.

"Sure," said Thalia.

"Everybody, everybody," called Mrs. Blair,

clapping her hands to rally the group. "Make a wide circle and we'll school to begin with. Horse's length apart. Walk on. Good striding walk."

They heard Mr. Knowles before they saw him.

"I told you you would be last. Always last. What's happened to you, boy? Anyone would think you couldn't ride. Go on. Thirty pounds it cost me to hire that horse, so get riding!"

They burst out of the leafy shelter of the lane, Dragonfly at a ragged trot, Simon sitting loosely in the saddle. Simon had turned his head away from his father, who was running at his side shouting.

"Simon, slot in behind Blackbird," said Mrs. Blair. "That's it."

*"Ride, boy! Ride!"* bawled Mr. Knowles.

There was an indrawn breath of irritation from the spectators. Tongues tutted as they turned to speak to each other.

"Wake him up," roared Mr. Knowles as Simon rode around, making no attempt to control Dragonfly.

"Prepare to halt. Halt," commanded Mrs.

Blair. She marched straight up to Mr. Knowles.

"If you cannot be quiet, kindly go back to your car and leave Simon with me."

"The lad's a wimp. . . ." began Mr. Knowles.

"If you please," insisted Mrs. Blair.

She was short and thickset, with large, flat eyes that glared up at Mr. Knowles's six-foot height. She waited until he turned unwillingly away to join the other parents.

Sally looked across the circle at Simon. If her father had ever behaved like that, she would have died or at least wanted the earth to open and swallow her up, but Simon was totally ignoring all the commotion. He was staring out over the hills while the chestnut Dragonfly fretted at his bit.

"Prepare to walk. Walk on," said Mrs. Blair.

Two middle-aged ladies crossed the field close to the group. As Sally rode past, she heard one lady say to the other:

"Tragic, really tragic. When you think what it all used to be like."

"And Simon! He used to be such a good rider, and now . . ."

"Sorry dear, sorry," said the other lady, catching Mrs. Blair's hard stare. They both scuttled off to join the other parents.

"Prepare to trot. Trot on," called Mrs. Blair, giving Sally no time to think about what she had overheard.

After they had schooled at a walk, trot, and canter, Mrs. Blair took them down to where there were four cross-country obstacles: two jumps made out of barrels, one with a pole on the far side; a dry stone wall; and a post-and-rails. They took turns jumping.

Willow popped neatly over all four jumps, taking them at a slow, steady canter. Sally managed to stay with her horse, making her feel fizzy with success. She rode back to the others, patting Willow's neck and praising her.

Tarquin plunged and soared over the jumps.

"Highflier!" exclaimed Mrs. Blair, but she didn't stop to listen to Thalia's explanations.

"Is that everyone? Everyone had a turn?"

"Simon!" roared Mr. Knowles. Simon, who had been hiding at the back of the other riders, walked reluctantly forward.

"Please, Simon," said Mrs. Blair, speaking

directly to Simon, who had turned his head away from her. "Do stop this silly nonsense. Now let me see you jumping. I know Dragonfly, he'll take you over these obstacles without a second thought."

Simon gathered his reins together and trotted Dragonfly in a circle. He turned toward the first jump and Dragonfly broke into a gallop, pounding up to the jump. At exactly the point where Dragonfly would have taken off, Simon pulled his horse to one side, forcing him to canter around the side of the jump.

"What on earth is he doing?" asked Thalia.

"He stopped him! He did it on purpose," said Sally. "Perhaps he's afraid of jumping."

But Simon did not look scared. His face was set in a bleak mask of determination.

"There," he said, riding back to Mrs. Blair. "I've jumped. That's it."

Mrs. Blair stepped toward him, opening her mouth as if she was going to speak. Then quite suddenly she stopped and came back to stand in front of the other riders.

"You all jumped well," she said. "Now everyone is going to go around again, and I want to see you letting your horses gallop on. Canter a circle first, and then ride the jumps as a course. Let your horses go on, taking the jumps in their stride. You are thinking of the whole course, not of four single jumps. Verity, take Buster around first. Remember to look up and think ahead."

Verity cantered in a wide circle, turned to the first jump, and let her horse gallop on.

Watching intently, Sally could see the difference in the way Verity was riding. As she landed from the first jump she was looking ahead to the second jump, riding on without hesitation.

Tarquin scorched around. Mrs. Blair said if he touched a fixed jump at that speed he would come down. She made Thalia jump again, steadying Tarquin to a canter.

"You see, he can jump perfectly well at that speed," said Mrs. Blair. "It is up to you to control him."

When it was Sally's turn, she could still picture Verity's round, how she had urged her horse on, riding smoothly, without hesitation. But when Sally came to the first jump, she just couldn't keep herself from steadying Willow to a collected canter, letting her pop neatly over the jump. Then, when she had landed safely, Sally rode her at the next jump doing exactly the same thing.

"Don't be afraid, dear," said Mrs. Blair sympathetically. "You must have confidence in your horse. She'll jump for you."

"We're jumping in the pairs at the show," interrupted Thalia.

"Really," said Mrs. Blair, as if she did not think it was a good idea.

This time Simon did not try to jump. Neither Mrs. Blair nor his father paid any attention to him. When Mrs. Blair led the way to the cross-country course, Simon dragged behind at the back of the group.

In spite of Thalia's pleading, Mrs. Blair let them tackle only five of the obstacles.

"But you saw him," pleaded Thalia. "You saw how he sailed over them. Please let me jump them all."

"Yes, I saw you. You must steady him up," said Mrs. Blair sharply. "School him at a sitting trot over cavaletti."

Thalia groaned and muttered.

Willow jumped the poles, the shrubbery, and

the barrels with Sally sitting balanced in the saddle. At the ditch-and-pole she was left behind, and Willow stopped at the next jump, waited until Sally got herself sorted out, then jumped it easily the second time.

"Not at all bad," said Mrs. Blair. "Don't be afraid to let Willow canter on. She'll jump if she possibly can. It was your fault that she stopped at the last jump. You were left behind. I think from the way she jumps she's been around a cross-country course before this. She'll look after you."

Sally nodded, knowing that what Mrs. Blair said was true. It was her fault. She hadn't let Willow gallop on.

"And if you are jumping in the pairs with Thalia, she is going to have to slow down and you must speed up. You'll both need to put in some hard work before the show. School together as a pair and then practice over broad, easy jumps, concentrating on keeping together as a pair."

Sally felt her heart sink. She was sure she would never dare to keep up with Thalia. For a second her old fear of being run away with lit up in her mind—Willow charging madly over rough hillside, crashing into jumps or falling while she sat helplessly, totally out of control.

"Stop it. Stop it at once," Sally told herself. "That's all past. Willow won't run away with you." She patted Willow's solid shoulder and smoothed down her silver mane. If she was riding Willow, she was safe.

"Does Simon want to jump?" asked Mrs. Blair when everyone else had been around the course.

"He'll jump," stated Mr. Knowles, running up to Simon and slapping Dragonfly on the quarters, flinging his arms wide to chase the horse on.

Before Mrs. Blair could do anything, Dragonfly had burst into a ragged canter and was charging up the hillside while Simon sat like a barnacle, his face expressionless.

Seeing the telephone poles in front of him and remembering how he had been pulled aside from the other jumps, the chestnut horse pricked his ears, snatched at his bit, and charged at the telephone poles.

"Jump it," roared Mr. Knowles. "Jump!"

Instantly Simon shortened his reins. Pulling with all his strength on his left rein, he fought to stop Dragonfly from reaching the jump.

The horse reared up in temper, struggling to free his head. He touched down and bucked wildly, but Simon, still looking as if nothing was happening, dug in his right heel tight and hard and jerked on the left rein, forcing Dragonfly to avoid the jump. The horse, pulled off balance, staggered and nearly fell.

"He'll end up killing the boy," said Martine Dawes as she watched Simon. "Wait till I tell Mr. Frazer about this."

"Why won't his father leave him alone?" demanded a watching father. "The boy does not want to jump. That is obvious."

"Well, he will *not* be hiring another horse from us," answered Martine. "Not if I have anything to do with it."

Dragonfly careened over the hillside, a bright flying shape completely out of control, with Simon sitting easily in the saddle.

"Simon, come back at once," called Mrs. Blair, with a despairing groan. "Simon, come back!"

But Simon showed no sign of hearing her.

"Would you take over?" Mrs. Blair asked Martine.

Martine nodded and began leading horses and riders back to the field.

Twisting around in her saddle, Sally saw Mrs. Blair march briskly toward Simon. Simon brought Dragonfly to a walk and, turning, began to ride back down the hill. When Sally lost sight of them, Mrs. Blair was standing beside them, her hand on Dragonfly's neck, talking earnestly to Simon.

## *Chapter Four*

By nine o'clock the next morning, Thalia and Sally were riding between the beech trees down the long drive from Kestrel Manor. They were going to find obstacles to jump. Before they had left Ashdale, Mrs. Blair, talking to all the children, had told them that between now and the show they were to pop their horses over anything small that could be jumped—a low place in a hedge, a dry stone wall, a fallen tree trunk—anything natural that their horses would be able to jump easily. Anything to get them used to jumping strange obstacles that they hadn't seen before.

Mrs. Blair had also talked about schooling at a sitting trot and jumping three low poles set in a schooling circle.

Thalia only remembered the jumping.

They rode across the sand dunes and over the shore to the rotting jetty.

"Mrs. Blair said to look carefully before we jump," cautioned Sally. "To make sure that the landing is okay."

"Not here," shouted Thalia, riding Tarquin at the jetty. "We know it's okay here."

"I was only telling you what Mrs. Blair said," insisted Sally, but Thalia was already jumping the jetty.

Sally gathered Willow together and jumped behind her.

"Now," Thalia said. "We'll trot in a circle, ride at the jetty together, and jump as a pair. Right?"

They trotted in a circle, turned toward the jetty, and instantly Tarquin tore at the jump, his racing hoofs winged with sand. He had landed far out on the other side before Willow had even taken off.

They jumped three more times, and each time the same thing happened.

"We are supposed to be a pair!" exclaimed Thalia. "I am not supposed to be leading you."

"Then don't," snapped Sally. "Keep him back with me. Willow won't go racing at a jump like an idiot, the way you do."

For a moment they stared at each other, on the verge of a fight.

It was Thalia who took off her hard hat,

shook out her sunburst of hair, and laughed.

"Let's find something else to jump," she said. "Tarquin knows ye ancient old jetties too well. He's too used to belting over them. Let's go and ask Mr. Palmer if we can jump over his farmland. He's friendly enough with Narg, so I think he'll let us."

But even when they had permission to ride on Mr. Palmer's land, they couldn't find much to jump. They had just finished dragging two empty hen coops into the middle of a field when Mrs. Palmer appeared at the field gate, yelling at them to put the coops back where they belonged.

"Not our day," muttered Thalia when they were riding away from the farm.

"Where are we going now?" asked Sally, thinking that perhaps they should go home and school as a pair over the jumps in the field.

"Sandwiches," said Thalia.

They found a trail leading over the hillside and rode along it until they came to a clear stream. They dismounted, loosened their girths, and let the horses drink. Then they sat down on the boulders at the side of the water, put their arms through their grazing horses' reins, and ate their sandwiches.

White clouds drifted over clear blue sky. Far above them the soaring silhouette of a buzzard rose and fell on currents of air.

"Why can't we just enjoy ourselves?" thought Sally. "It's all perfect the way it is. Horses and being happy. If it wasn't for this jumping we could just be here." Willow's enormous head loomed over her shoulder, searching for tidbits.

"We could just stay here," Sally said aloud.

"I've got an idea," Thalia announced, springing to her feet, ignoring Sally. "We'll ride up to the Moss. There are plenty of stone walls there. And they're at the right height for us to practice going over as a pair."

Sally tugged up Willow's girth and mounted. She knew there was something she had heard about the Moss, some warning about riding there, but she couldn't quite remember what it was.

"We can go on along this trail," said Thalia, riding on confidently. "I don't know why I didn't think about the Moss before." She glanced out of the corner of her eye at Sally, checking to see what she was thinking.

They followed the trail for about half an hour, then rode along a broader, tree-lined path.

"Nearly there," said Thalia as they left the lane. Spreading out before them was a wide reach of flat, open land. On the left was a stretch of water overgrown with reeds. Whitewashed farmhouses were scattered about the sloping green fields, and on the right was the garden of a small stone cottage with two stalls and an overgrown paddock.

Thalia trotted ahead until they passed the garden, where rough grass crisscrossed by dry stone walls began.

"Wow!" gasped Sally. "What a perfect place to ride. Why haven't we ever come here before?"

But Thalia didn't answer. She was already cantering across the grass and jumping Tarquin over a low wall.

"You can jump where you like," shouted Thalia. "Come on."

At first Sally checked cautiously, peering over walls to make sure there were no fallen stones on the landing side. But even when Willow's hoofs clattered on fallen stones, it didn't seem to make any difference to her; she never felt like she was about to fall. Thalia's recklessness, and Willow's pricked ears and dancing hooves, filled Sally with delight. She completely forgot her fears. Like Thalia, she galloped over the small fields, leaping over the walls in an ecstasy of freedom.

"There's a better wall farther on," said Thalia, her eyes bright. Tarquin's arched neck and stamping hooves demanded more galloping, more jumping. "Down this way."

They rode down the hillside to the track, Willow following Tarquin, making high pig squeals of excitement. Thalia let Tarquin gallop on until they reached a stone wall that ran between the track and the water. It was about two feet high. The land between the wall and the water was short, rough grass.

"You can jump it anywhere," cried Thalia as she swung Tarquin off the track to the right and turned him to jump the wall.

But Sally didn't follow her. There was something not right about the ground on the other side. Somehow the grass looked too smooth, too bright.

Tarquin plunged at the wall. Sally saw him soar out and land. Only he didn't land. He sank through the ground, his legs vanishing instantly, his belly, chest, and quarters sinking more slowly out of sight.

Sally's cries mingled with Tarquin's high, terrible screaming.

In a split second Thalia had torn off her jacket, thrown it across the grass toward the wall, and—squirming her legs free from the bog—launched herself onto it. With a convulsive struggle she reached the firm ground by the wall. Her left hand was clenched on the buckle of Tarquin's reins.

"Get help! Get help!" she cried, but already Sally was galloping full out, back to the cottage. As she bent low over Willow's neck, she could see nothing but Tarquin's reaching neck, bursting eyeballs, and screaming nostrils.

A wicker gate in the garden hedge was open. Sally stormed through it and galloped to the door. Leaping from Willow, she pressed her finger on the bell and kept it there.

To Sally's utter astonishment it was Mr. Knowles who came to the door.

"What the—" he began.

"There's a horse in the swamp. He's in right up to his neck. Quick! Quick! You've got to do something!"

A gray-haired woman in a floral dress had followed Mr. Knowles to the door.

"I'll phone Alan Campbell," she said. "Get him to bring his tractor and a rope. I just hope he's in."

Sally was leaning against the door, tears pouring down her face.

In minutes the woman was back.

"He's coming at once," she said. "We'd better get to them."

The woman ran across the garden and picked up a bike that was leaning against a garden seat.

Simon was standing at the foot of the stairs. Sally did not know how long he had been there or what he had heard.

"A tractor's no use," he said urgently. "It'll sink. You've got to get a backhoe. There's one digging a ditch at Carruth Farm."

But Mr. Knowles rushed past him. Sally, too, turned Willow and, springing onto her, galloped back to Thalia and Tarquin.

When Sally reached them, the floral lady had her arm around Thalia's shoulders. Like some weird statue, Tarquin's head and neck were still above the swamp ground. Thalia's hand was still tightly clenched on Tarquin's reins.

Mr. Knowles reached them next, carrying a rough rope halter and blankets.

"Still with us?" he asked, staring at Tarquin's head. "Looks as if he's got his feet on a bank of firm ground. All depends on how long that will hold."

Thalia's face was clenched shut, all her will centered on Tarquin.

"Here," said Mr. Knowles, tossing the rope halter to Thalia. "You're the lightest. Lie down flat where your jacket is and see if you can get this around his head. They'll never pull him out by those reins."

Thalia lay flat on the ground, the floral lady holding one foot, Mr. Knowles the other, and began to squirm over her jacket toward Tarquin. He rolled his eyes and laid back his ears as Thalia lassoed the halter over his head. With shaking hands she managed to tie a knot in it. Then, holding tightly on to the rope,

Thalia allowed herself to be pulled back to firm ground.

They waited in silence, trying not to stare at Tarquin but hardly able to take their eyes off him.

"The tractor!" cried Thalia, her eager ears hearing it first.

The tractor bounced toward them, its huge wheels rumbling over the rough track.

"Who got the horse stuck in there?" demanded Alan Campbell, driving right up to them and jumping down. "If you kids would keep off my land . . . How often have you been told that it's too swampy to ride on?"

He took the rope from Thalia. Going as close to Tarquin as he could, he tried to pull at his head, but with no effect.

"Can't do anything from here," he said, dragging his boots free from the swamp and coming back to them. "I need to try and get down closer to him. See if I can get a pull on him from there. He's in deep. I don't know if I can do anything."

Alan Campbell backed his tractor to the end of the wall and drove off the track. For a second the giant wheels advanced over the bright grass, then slowly they sank into the swamp. He was held prisoner as fatally as Tarquin.

They all stared at the stationary tractor in fascinated horror. What could they do now? A dry, cracked sound came from the base of Thalia's throat, and she began to shake uncontrollably.

Sally stared at Tarquin. She was sure she saw his neck sink deeper into the swamp.

The adults talked in quick, desperate voices. Mr. Knowles got on the bike to go and phone the police. The floral lady tried to wrap a blanket around Thalia. Sally bit hard on her knuckles to keep herself from screaming. She could not believe that this nightmare was real.

There was a clonking and shuddering that shook the ground, startling them all, as down the trail came a backhoe.

Thalia shook herself free from the floral lady's blanket. She sprang to her feet.

"He's here," she cried. "Oh, quick, quick. Hurry."

The man driving the backhoe was tall and broad-shouldered, with a mop of white curls. He jolted the backhoe to a shuddering halt and, sucking through his teeth, sized up the situation. He exchanged a few muttered words with the young man who was with him. The young man climbed into the bucket at the end of the backhoe's long crane arm and was swung out above Tarquin's head.

No one spoke. They all watched in terrified silence as the young man hooked up the halter rope. He fixed it securely to the backhoe and, inch by desperate inch, the backhoe began to haul Tarquin from the swamp.

At first only his head and neck moved, stretching out as Tarquin was dragged forward. Sally was sure that the rope would snap; Thalia certain that Tarquin's neck would be broken.

Relentlessly the backhoe dragged Tarquin forward. His shoulders burst free from the swamp, but he gave no sign of life. For minutes that seemed like hours, like days, they watched Tarquin being dragged forward until at last he lay on solid ground, a huge bulk of swamped horse.

Thalia, who had never taken her eyes off Tarquin for a second, threw herself down at his head. She crouched beside him, pulling his ears through her hands, whispering his name and talking to him. For minutes he lay without any sign of life. Then his ear twitched.

"He's not dead," cried Thalia. "He's not dead!" Almost as if he had understood her words, Tarquin surged to his feet, stood uncertainly, then shook himself, globs of swamp flying from him. Then, to everyone's delight, he took a few steps forward and began to graze as if nothing had happened.

"How on earth did you know we were here?" Mr. Knowles asked the backhoe driver.

"A boy phoned Carruth. Bob came out shouting that it was urgent, so I came straightaway. Not the first beast I've pulled out of that bog. It's a dangerous place."

Thalia threw muddied arms around his neck and kissed him.

"Now," she said, "I know what the angel Gabriel will look like."

"It was Simon who phoned," said Sally. "He said we needed a backhoe, that a tractor would be no use. But no one paid any attention to him."

"Where is he now?" barked Mr. Knowles.

"Skulking in the house. Should have been out here giving us a hand. Useless boy!"

They went back to the Knowleses' cottage while Mr. Knowles phoned Kestrel Manor and arranged with a horrified Mrs. Lorimer about paying for the use of the tractor and the backhoe. Thalia and Sally tried to wash some of the swamp off Tarquin in the yard, drank the hot sweet tea the floral lady had made for them, and thanked Mr. Knowles.

"I must thank Simon too," Thalia insisted. "He thought of the backhoe. I've got to thank him."

But Mr. Knowles had turned back to the house without answering Thalia. The floral lady said not to worry, that she would tell Simon.

The girls left the house by the side gate, Sally riding Willow and Thalia leading Tarquin.

"You'd think he would have called Simon so I could thank him," said Thalia.

Her face was chalk white, and she walked with an arm over Tarquin's withers. Tarquin, in spite of his ordeal, was walking along without any sign of lameness, his eyes bright and his face alert.

From one of the upstairs windows of the cottage, a boy looked down at them—straight wing of blond hair, dark eyes, and fixed, unyielding mouth.

"Simon!" yelled Thalia, waving her arms. "Come down. I want to thank you. Thank you for saving Tarquin."

But with a twitch of the curtain Simon was gone.

"Why didn't he come down?" demanded Sally.

"Too late now," said Thalia. "That motor-bike you can hear is Narg coming to find out what's been happening. There is going to be big trouble."

## *Chapter Five*

Thalia was right. There was big trouble, both from her narg and Sally's parents. Words like *foolish*, *irresponsible*, and *stupid* were used a lot. In the end they had to promise never to jump over anything unless there was an adult with them or the jump was on Kestrel Manor's grounds and had been seen by Mr. or Mrs. Lorimer.

"Never?" cried Thalia in dismay.

"Well, not until you are much older," said her narg.

The next morning when Thalia led Tarquin around the field he was still perfectly sound.

"I'll come over when I'm back from the dentist's torture chamber," she announced. "It'll be about four. They can both have a day of rest."

Left alone, Sally was bored. She brushed the Beardies and tidied her bedroom, then hung about the kitchen pestering her mother.

"We're going shopping," said Mrs. Lorimer,

holding Jamie by one hand and shopping bags in the other. "Are you coming?"

"Ice cream," said Jamie. "I'm having spider flavor. There's dead fly, squashed worm, or mouse tail."

Sally resisted the temptation.

When they were gone, she wandered down to the horses' field again and leaned on the gate, watching them grazing.

The nightmare picture of Tarquin vanishing into the swamp was still vivid in her mind.

If Simon hadn't phoned for the backhoe, it would have been too late, she thought. Too late for any of us to have phoned. By that time Tarquin would have been swallowed up by the swamp. She shuddered, remembering clearly how she had seen Tarquin's neck sinking deeper into the bog.

Although Sally had agreed with Thalia that it would be a good idea to give the horses a rest day, she decided that it wouldn't do Willow any harm to ride her along the beach—just for half an hour at a walk.

She took Meg with her and rode slowly along the shore, thinking about Simon. It was strange the way he wouldn't jump. He didn't seem to want to ride at all. Yet when Dragonfly had been galloping and bucking his way over the hillside, Simon had stayed on effortlessly.

Sally tried to remember what the women had said to each other. Something about it all being tragic.

Tragic? Sally thought, wondering what could have happened to Simon. Something so bad that people called it tragic.

Meg trotted along beside Willow, carrying a lump of driftwood in her mouth.

"You are the best dog," Sally told her. "The best dog in the world." Meg looked up at her, smiling with her eyes, wagging her tail.

Sally had never known life without Meg. Meg had been two when Sally was born. She had always been there. Last year she would have been racing over the beach, digging in the sand, rolling in the seaweed, chasing gulls, but now her age had slowed her down, clouded her eyes, and stiffened her joints. Sally swallowed hard and steadied Willow to a halt. Meg dropped her lump of wood and sat down panting, glad of the rest.

The tide was far out, the wet sands gleaming.

Sally touched her reins and let Willow walk on toward a black castle of rock, close to the sea's edge. Meg picked up her driftwood and followed behind.

They had almost reached the mass of rock when Meg ran ahead, her barking muffled through her lump of wood. She went right up to the rock, dropped the driftwood, and stepped back barking furiously, asking whoever was there to throw it for her.

Sally squinted against the sun but could see no one. She shouted to Meg to behave herself and rode toward the rock. There, hidden by a cleft in the rock, staring out to sea, was a boy with straight blond hair.

"Simon!" Sally exclaimed in amazement. "Why are you here?" Then, realizing that it wasn't any of her business, she shouted at Meg to be quiet.

"Anyway," she went on, "I'm very glad you *are* here. We want to thank you for yesterday. For phoning for the backhoe. You saved Tarquin."

Simon took Meg's lump of wood and threw it out to sea. Meg ran after it.

"It's okay," said Simon, still not looking at Sally. "I remembered last time, when they were trying to get a sheep out. The tractor got stuck and the sheep went down. Even when you know the Moss well, it's dangerous. Dad's getting the farmer to put up warning signs."

"But *you* remembered. *You* phoned the farm. It was *you* who saved Tarquin."

Meg dumped her driftwood back at Simon's feet. As he bent down to throw it for her again, Sally saw that his face was streaked with tears. Obviously Simon had come out here to be alone. She thought of riding away, saying good-bye, and pretending that she hadn't noticed—but she couldn't. Simon must be really miserable to be sitting here alone crying.

"What's wrong?" Sally asked, sliding down from Willow. "Can we help—I mean, Thalia and me? We'd both do anything to help because of you saving Tarquin. Honestly, anything."

Simon turned his head away.

"I don't need help," he said. But the next second he had dropped his head into his hands and was crying bitterly.

Sally waited, fiddling with Willow's mane

until Simon stopped crying, dried his eyes, and blew his nose.

"Sorry," he said. "Didn't mean to carry on like that. It's just that everything's so hopeless. Dad shouting like an idiot all the time. But I don't care. I am never going to jump again. Not ever."

"Are you scared?" asked Sally sympathetically. "Before I got Willow I was scared of galloping, and even now I'm not all that good at jumping."

"Of course I'm not scared," said Simon. "I've won cups, and lots of ribbons. But it makes sense, doesn't it, when you've killed your horse and broken your legs. You don't want to go and do the same thing again, do you? That makes sense, doesn't it?"

"Did you?" demanded Sally, hardly able to take in what Simon had told her.

"I was riding in hunter trials, going too fast because I had to make up time. I knew it was risky, but I was sure Merlin could do it. And he could have, but he slipped on the takeoff. His leg got caught up on the fixed poles. He broke it and I came off and broke both of mine. They took me to the hospital, but they put him down. When they patched my bones together and let me go home, all Dad would do was shout at me to ride again. At first I wouldn't ride at all. Then I gave in and rode at Pony Club things, on Mr. Frazer's horses. But that wasn't enough. Now it's shout, shout, shout at me to jump. You heard him. But I won't. I won't."

"Dragonfly nearly did," said Sally.

Simon nodded, shivering suddenly.

"Mr. Frazer said that he wasn't letting Dad hire any more of his horses; that I was ruining them. So now Dad's going to buy one. I can't stop him. That's where we should be today, only I managed to dodge out and come here."

"But don't you want a horse?" asked Sally in amazement. "Even when I was having nightmares about galloping, I still wanted a horse!"

"Not the kind of horse Dad will buy. It will be a crazy chestnut like that Dragonfly. Wanting to do nothing else but jump and jump. It'll always be there in Merlin's stall, reminding me of Merlin, and someday it will all happen again. I know it will."

"What about your mom?"

"That was Aunt Dot you saw yesterday. Mom was killed in a car crash about a month before my fall," said Simon, his voice flat and distant as an old recording that had been played over and over again.

"Oh," said Sally, having no words, suddenly understanding what the women had meant by tragic.

"So you see we're a has-been family."

"But if you had a horse like Willow . . ." said Sally, returning to the only part of Simon's story that she really understood.

"I just don't want a horse. Anyway, Dad wouldn't buy a quiet, sensible horse. He wants to see me back at the top."

"I bet you he would," said Sally. "I bet if you said that you'd ride a quiet horse, he would buy one for you just so you would start riding again."

Simon shrugged. "Where would he find one to buy? The show's on Saturday. He knows about this horse that's fast and a brilliant jumper. That's the one we were going to see." Simon sat staring out to sea, ignoring Meg's barking demand to throw her driftwood, ignoring Sally and Willow, staring hopelessly in front of him.

Although Simon had said he wasn't scared, Sally thought he was. Not nervous the way she was, but afraid to jump again after his accident. If he had a quiet horse, she thought, a horse that was his own, he would get to know her. He'd start riding again because he would want to, and that would be a beginning.

The noise Sally made was something like a hundred express trains coming out of a hundred tunnels. It made Meg bark more furiously than ever; it made the gulls at the sea's edge flock up in clamorous clouds; it made Willow start and Simon jump to his feet.

"But of course," cried Sally. "You can buy Clover. She wouldn't jump! Not in a million years. Clover would be just the horse for you!"

## *Chapter Six*

"Yes, I still have Clover," said Miss Meek's voice on the phone. "Yes, I suppose she's still for sale. Why? Have you changed your mind?"

"Not for me," said Sally. "Someone else. Could they come out tomorrow afternoon to see her? And could I come out in the morning with a friend to dress her up a bit?"

"Well," said Miss Meek in a surprised voice. "I suppose you could. We'd all love to see you again."

Sally went back to the living room, where her family and Thalia were waiting to hear the result of her phone call. "Miss Meek will be pleased to see us, and Clover is still for sale."

At first Simon had insisted that he did not want any kind of horse.

"But if your father says that you must have one, why not buy Clover? I promise you she is totally, one-hundred-percent jump-proof. Nothing would make Clover run away. Absolutely nothing would make her jump. At least persuade your father to go and see her."

"If you can fix it, I'll go and look at her," Simon had said at last, getting to his feet, throwing Meg's driftwood for the last time. "Honestly, I do not want a horse. I do not want to ride, but I suppose it would make life easier if I do."

Yet as he walked away, he had called back over his shoulder, "See you tomorrow." And he had grinned at Sally, a sudden smile lighting up his bleak face.

"Now," said Sally, standing behind her father's chair and wrapping her arms around his neck. "It's your turn."

When Sally's parents had heard the story of Simon's accident, they both agreed that Clover would be a quiet, steady horse for him. Mr. Lorimer had reluctantly agreed to call Mr. Knowles, telling him that he knew of a suitable horse for his son.

"Sound horsey," encouraged Mrs. Lorimer as her husband got to his feet. "A man who knows a good horse when he sees one."

"I'll speak to him if you like," offered Thalia,

but Sally was already dialing Simon's number.

Simon answered.

"It's Sally. Dad is here to speak to your father. Clover is still for sale."

"A thoroughly decent horse. Totally trustworthy. Just the thing for your son," Mr. Lorimer assured Mr. Knowles, while Mrs. Lorimer buried her face in a cushion to keep her giggling from being heard on the other end of the phone.

"They're going to see Clover tomorrow afternoon about three. He was a bit suspicious about Miss Meek's riding school. Said he'd never heard of it. But I talked him around," Mr. Lorimer told them, feeling pleased with himself.

The next morning Mr. Lorimer gave Sally and Thalia a lift to the riding school on his way to work. They had gotten up early and practiced jumping as a pair in the paddock, though really it had not been jumping together, more Tarquin leading Willow over the jumps.

"Hope they buy her," said Mr. Lorimer before he drove away. "I'd like to see her in a good home. Always felt it was a bit miserable turning her down like that. Anyway, good luck." He drove away to his library.

"Pretty pathetic," said Thalia, looking around at Miss Meek's house, stabling, and fields wired off into grazing strips. "Is that the lane where you rode? Wasn't it deadly boring?"

"I suppose so," said Sally, realizing how much she had changed and how incredibly lucky she was to have all the freedom of Kestrel Manor and Willow to ride.

Quickly Sally crossed the yard, peering into familiar stalls. Well-loved faces looked out over half-doors or turned in their stalls to see her—Tansy, Mint, Amber, Prince, and Princess. Sally fed them sliced carrots from the bag she had brought with her, scratched necks, patted shoulders, but Clover wasn't there.

"She must be out," said Sally, and they ran around the stabling to the grazing strips.

"Clover," called Sally. "Clover!"

The black horse with the white socks was nibbling at the short grass, her rump turned toward Sally.

"Clover!" she called again. This time Clover heard her and swung around. She stood for a moment, her ears curious, her eyes questioning. Then, with a welcoming whinny, she trotted straight up to Sally.

"She knows me! She remembered me!" cried Sally, throwing her arms over Clover's rough neck and straggling mane. "She knew it was me!"

"She's not much to look at," said Thalia critically. "D'you think Mr. Knowles will want to buy her?"

"He *has to,*" insisted Sally.

Now that she had seen Clover again, Sally could not bear the thought of leaving her behind in the riding school for a second time. Even if she did look a bit poor and overworked, she would be the best possible horse for Simon. Clover would never jump, and that was what Simon wanted.

Miss Meek asked them in for lemonade and cookies. She questioned Sally about Kestrel Manor and Willow. Thalia told her about Tarquin. Then Miss Meek asked them about the family who was interested in Clover.

"They've got two stalls and the boy who will ride her is a very good rider. He just wants a horse to ride around on. She would have a really good home," Sally told her.

"Wish someone would give me a really good home," said Miss Meek, setting her empty coffee mug on the table and standing up. "But seeing that that's not likely to happen, I'd better go on and do some work. You can bring Clover in and brush her down. You remember where the brushes are kept?"

Clover stood like a wooden horse in the center of the stall while Sally and Thalia brushed out her mane and tail, washed her white socks, and worked on her coat with a dandy brush until it was nearly shining.

As she groomed, the lump in Sally's throat grew bigger. She *so* wanted Clover to go home with Simon. She could not bear the thought of her being left at Miss Meek's.

"There," said Thalia, standing back and looking at Clover. "Not quite a silk purse, but less of a sow's ear. Let's eat."

Thalia refilled the water bucket. When Clover had finished drinking, Sally tipped a feed of pony nuts, which she had brought from Kestrel Manor, into Clover's manger. Then they sat outside, leaning against the stall door eating their sandwiches and waiting for Simon.

Mr. Knowles's low-slung scarlet sports car swept into the yard, pulling a single horse trailer behind it. Instantly everything in the yard seemed shabbier, more run-down, than ever. Simon was sitting next to his father, staring out the car window with his usual withdrawn air. Aunt Dot sat in the back.

"Hi," called Thalia, jumping up and racing toward the car. "We've got Clover ready for you, and thank you, thank you, thank you for saving Tarquin. Thank you, thank you for thinking of the backhoe. Absolutely any time you want to ride Tarquin, he is yours."

Simon shrugged his way out of the car and said it was okay, while his father got out and stared around the yard.

"What a dump," he shouted.

And Sally knew that Miss Meek must have heard him as she came across the yard toward them.

"We forgot to clean the tack," whispered

Thalia as Miss Meek saddled and bridled Clover with a dry, cracked bridle and sweat-stained saddle.

But when Clover was led out of the box, she didn't look too old or too thin. A sudden burst of sunlight made her eyes gleam and her coat shimmer. So for a moment she almost looked like the kind of horse that Mr. Knowles might buy for his son. Almost.

"Well, if it's an old scarecrow like this that you want to ride, let's see you on it. *Simon! Wake up!* Get on with it, boy."

"She isn't a scarecrow, and she isn't old," said Sally. "She's a good horse. She was my horse when I rode here. . . ." But no one was paying any attention to her.

Miss Meek had tightened Clover's girth, and Simon was mounting.

"We ride in the lane," Miss Meek said. With her hand on Clover's bit-ring she began to walk toward the lane.

"She knows Clover will try to bolt back to her stall," Sally thought.

"Let him go," ordered Mr. Knowles. "The boy can ride, you know."

"Keep an eye on her," Miss Meek warned Simon, but she let go of the bit and walked in front of Clover.

The instant Miss Meek let go of her, Clover stopped dead.

Sally's nails bit into the palms of her hands. "If Clover carts him back to the stall, Mr. Knowles will never buy her," she thought.

Clover dropped her head, shied suddenly sideways, ready to spin around and bolt.

"Watch out!" yelled Thalia.

But in an instant, without appearing to do anything, no kicking, no yanking at his reins, Simon had Clover gathered together and trotting after Miss Meek.

Simon rode Clover up and down the lane in the same way. He seemed to do nothing, but Clover changed from a walk to a trot, from a trot to a canter and back, as if she were a dressage horse. Sally knew then that Simon hadn't just been showing off when he had told her that he had won ribbons and cups. Simon really could ride.

"I've never seen Clover go so well for any

child," Miss Meek said to Mr. Knowles as they watched.

"Oh, he was a very good little rider," said Aunt Dot, who had squeezed herself out of the back of the car to join them. "We were all so proud of him."

"Boy refuses to ride, that's the shame of it," said Mr. Knowles. "Stubborn as a mule. Can't do a thing with him."

Simon rode back to the yard at an extended walk.

"Well?" demanded his father.

Waiting for Simon's reply, Sally held her breath, seeing Clover grazing in the paddock beside the Knowleses' house or being led back to her grazing strip while the Knowleses drove away.

Simon dismounted.

"I don't want a horse," he said, "but if you must buy me a horse, I suppose it may as well be Clover."

"We'll take her on trial," said Mr. Knowles. "The boy can ride her at the show on Saturday?"

Mr. Knowles and Miss Meek arranged deposit and price.

"I'm so glad you're taking her," cried Sally. "She won't jump. You don't need to worry; I know she won't jump."

"I felt a lot better on her than I ever did on those runaways that Dad was always hiring from Mr. Frazer. Perhaps he'll leave me alone now. Perhaps it will satisfy him if I just ride around on Clover." Simon smiled suddenly, giving Clover a fruit drop from his pocket and scratching under her mane. "You can be my horse and there won't be any more fights."

"I cannot imagine," said Thalia as she and Sally rode home in the backseat of Mr. Lorimer's car, "how he could possibly have chosen Clover when his dad would have bought him any horse he wanted. Why doesn't he want a decent horse?"

"I told you about the accident," said Sally.

"Oh, I know! But to buy a horse like Clover!"

Sally didn't answer. She sat next to Thalia, filled with happiness. No longer would the thought of Clover being left behind at Miss Meek's riding school haunt her dreams.

"And that's another day wasted when we

should have been schooling," moaned Thalia. "We've hardly practiced jumping as a pair. Hardly at all. And not tomorrow but the next day is the show!"

## Chapter Seven

The next morning Sally and Thalia brought in their horses, fed them, and left them with an armful of hay each. Then they went down to the field to build cross-country obstacles.

"Four will be enough," said Thalia, dragging out a broken branch from under the chestnut tree. "Make them wide so we can practice jumping together. That's what we've got to practice, jumping as a pair."

"You don't say," muttered Sally under her breath.

"Like Mrs. Blair said, you've got to wake Willow up. It is a pairs competition we're riding in!"

Sally stopped piling jumping poles into a solid mass.

"I do know," she said, scowling at Thalia. "I heard Mrs. Blair too. And I heard what she told you. You have to hold Tarquin back."

"Then where would we be? Not jumping anything! In a mess! I have got to ride Tarquin on and you have got to make Willow keep up with him. That is, *if* you want to win. *If* we are trying to win the cup, you have got to keep up with me. Right?"

For a second Sally stared at Thalia, on the edge of telling her just what she thought of her bossiness, but before she had gathered her words together, Thalia barreled on.

"Brainwave," she shouted. "I've got an idea. There's that old bench in the summerhouse. It would make a jump. Let's get it."

Ben, walking Meg and Misty, saw them struggling to carry the bench back to the field and came to help. In an hour they had created four reasonably solid jumps, all wide enough to be jumped as a pair.

After breakfast they rode down to the field. Sally was in a black mood. All through breakfast Thalia had gone on and on about how to ride a cross-country course and how important it was to go around at a good gallop.

"You'd think she was Mrs. Blair," Sally thought. "Knowing everything. Always right. Boss, boss, bossing."

They schooled first, riding in circles at a walk and sitting trot. Sally's bad temper ran down her reins, making Willow balk and shy at nothing. She walked with her head down, dragging her hooves and stumbling over tufts of grass.

"Oh, go on," Sally told her. "Willow, walk on." She tugged at her reins, kicking Willow on, knowing that in a minute Thalia would be organizing them into jumping. Never had Sally felt less like jumping. She knew she would be left behind, knew she would fall off. Suddenly she wondered what Simon was doing, wondered if he would be schooling, or sitting in his bedroom worrying about tomorrow.

"Better if we each have a jump around first," said Thalia. Tarquin flew over the obstacles like a guided missile. Willow trotted and stopped, trotted and stopped. Then, on her third attempt, she got in too close and shot over the jump from a standstill, throwing Sally onto her neck and depositing her onto the ground on the other side.

"What a beginning," moaned Thalia in despair. "What's Mrs. Blair going to think of us if you jump like that tomorrow?"

Remounting, Sally ignored her completely.

It was the middle of the afternoon when Mrs. Lorimer and Jamie came to see how they were doing. They were just in time to see Tarquin crash his way through the jumps while Willow, trotting well behind him, refused at the second and third jump and ran out at the fourth.

"That's useless," cried Thalia, not seeing Mrs. Lorimer and Jamie. "How can we go to Tarent tomorrow and botch the whole thing up like that? It's you!"

"Are you supposed to be a pair?" called Mrs. Lorimer, taking in the bored, cross horses, Thalia's temper, and Sally's silence.

"Yes, we were. Huh. Some pair," snorted Thalia, not caring that it was Sally's mother she was speaking to.

"You don't think," said Mrs. Lorimer, "that you've entered for the wrong class? Why on earth did you choose to enter a pairs class?"

"Seemed a good idea at the time," muttered Thalia.

"Can't you change your entry?"

"No way," snapped Thalia. "We've just got to go on trying to make them into a pair." She swung Tarquin around, ready to jump again.

"I don't think so," said Mrs. Lorimer in her most adult voice. "You've been jumping all day. No wonder they're fed up. Put them in their stalls and give them a rest."

"We've forgotten everything that Martine taught us," said Sally as she led Willow back to the stables. "Not only me, but you too."

"This is cross-country, not namby-pamby show jumping."

"We have to show jump too," exclaimed Sally, suddenly remembering.

"But it is the cross-country that really matters."

"Oh, I know, I know. Don't keep going on!"

"Sorry," said Thalia, not meaning it. "Sorry I spoke."

While they drank lemonade and ate Mrs. Lorimer's cherry cake, Sally and Thalia didn't speak to each other. Thalia played noisily with the Beardies. Sally stared out the kitchen window at the long glimmering line of the sea.

In the early evening, before they turned the horses out, they jumped over the battered obstacles one last time. Although Sally did her best to keep Willow up with Tarquin, he stormed ahead of her, his speed mocking Willow's neat, precise jumping.

"Better clean our tack," said Thalia scornfully. "Then they won't be able to say it's as bad as our jumping."

As they stood in the tack room, dragging wet sponges down sweaty reins, rubbing in the sharp-smelling saddle soap, polishing bits and stirrups, the silence between them settled into politeness.

"Please pass the saddle soap."

"Excuse me, could I have that sponge when you've finished with it?"

And even when Thalia upset the bucket of water, Sally didn't giggle as she usually would have. She just went on cleaning her saddle without looking around.

"Seven tomorrow morning?" said Thalia when all their tack was clean and the stalls brushed out.

"Yes," said Sally, wanting to stand and chat, wanting to talk about the show, about seeing Verity Blair again, about Simon and Clover.

But Thalia was already marching away, her shoulders squared, her head held high.

"Are you two still quarreling?" asked Mrs. Lorimer as Sally came into the kitchen. "What's it all about?"

"Nothing," said Sally automatically.

"Seems like more than nothing to me," said her mother. "Simon's father is on the phone. Your dad's speaking to him."

Sally hurried into the hall. Sitting on the bottom step of the stairs, she listened to her father saying, "Yes, of course. Yes. That would be no trouble at all. I'm sure the girls wouldn't mind in the least. Sally's here now. Do you want to speak to her? She knows more about the horse side of things than I do." Saying goodbye, he handed the receiver to Sally.

"Hello," said Mr. Knowles, his voice loud but not shouting. "We're having a bit of trouble here. Our trailer has cracked a wheel shaft, so the boy will have to ride to the show. I want to arrange it so he meets you two. Make sure he gets there. Doesn't go running off."

"We're riding there," said Sally. "Of course we can meet him."

"There's a crossroads about two miles from the show ground. Buxton's Free Range Eggs on one corner, Manor House Hotel on the other."

"Thalia will know."

"Right. That's fixed, then. Ten o'clock?"

"Yes," said Sally, hoping it would fit in with Thalia's schedule.

"Bye," said Mr. Knowles.

"Clover?" demanded Sally. "How is Clover? Has she settled in? Are you keeping her?"

"Depends what sort of performance they put on tomorrow. I've arranged for Simon to ride in the Handy Horse. Then we'll see about settling in or not. Here's Simon. Ask him."

"Yes," Simon said when Sally repeated her question. "She seems fine."

"We're going to meet you tomorrow."

"If I'm there," Simon said. Sally couldn't tell whether his voice was frightened or joking.

"Of course you'll be there. You *must* ride in the Handy Horse, or your father will send Clover back. Of course you're coming."

But Simon only said good-bye and hung up.

Sally's mother came to say good night. She

told her to hurry up and get into bed and not to worry about tomorrow.

For a long time Sally sat on the window seat, staring out over the sea. Clouds gusting over the full moon made it race across the sky, made the sea shimmer and her crystal unicorn sparkle with moonlight.

Suddenly Sally had the peculiar feeling that if she went down to the horses' field, Thalia would be there and they could make up. Pulling on her jacket, Sally crept through the dark house and picked her way through pits of moon shadow, down to the field.

But there was no one there. Only Tarquin and Willow lying by the looped branches of the chestnut tree.

Sally leaned on the field gate, swallowing back her disappointment, gazing at Tarquin's dark bulk and Willow's pale whiteness.

This time tomorrow it would all be over. No matter what happened, it would be over. But Sally didn't want it to be over; she wanted to be in the middle of it, in the middle of a day of winning and jumping, being with Thalia and

Simon, a day to equal her imagination, a day that would go on and on forever.

"If it's anything like today," Sally thought as she turned to walk slowly back to Kestrel Manor, "it will be a disaster. A total, absolute disaster."

## *Chapter Eight*

Sally's stomach was churning when she woke. Today was the Tarent show. Today she was going to show jump and ride cross-country. And yesterday she had quarreled with Thalia. She lay flat on her back, staring up at the white ceiling. It was Thalia's fault as much as her own, Tarquin's as much as Willow's. Thalia would need to hold him back, steady him, if they were ever going to jump as a pair.

Then Sally remembered Simon—that he was riding Clover in the Handy Horse, that he had to do well or his father would send Clover back to Miss Meek's, and that they had to meet him.

"If he comes at all," Sally thought, jumping out of bed. "But he must, and he must do well. Clover must never go back to Miss Meek's."

By the time Sally reached the stables, Thalia had brought in both horses.

"Narg says I have to apologize."

"Mom said the same thing. We've to stop being so stupid."

"Right," said Thalia. "Forget it. Okay?"

"Forgotten," said Sally.

"Absolutely," said Thalia. But it wasn't.

"Mr. Knowles phoned Dad last night," said Sally, the words rushing out of her to fill up the bad-tempered space that was still between them. "Their trailer has broken down, so we have to meet Simon at ten o'clock by a free-range–egg farm and a hotel. I said you'd know where it was."

"Oh, no!" groaned Thalia. "Why didn't you say we'd see him at the show? It's always such a mess meeting someone like that. If they're not there, you never know what's happened to them."

"I would think," said Sally before she could stop herself, "when someone had saved your horse from being sucked down into a swamp you wouldn't care how long you had to wait for him."

"It spoils everything," sulked Thalia. "Suppose we meet Verity. She won't want to hang around waiting, and Tarquin will be fed up if we have to wait. It'll put him in a bad mood for the day."

"Any minute now," thought Sally irritably, "she'll be telling me to keep up with her in the pairs." She left Thalia grumbling to herself while she started work on Willow's mane and tail.

By half past nine they were riding down the tree-shaded drive from Kestrel Manor to the main road. Their horses were groomed to perfection, manes and tails catching the breeze like silken strands, coats gleaming, their polished tack shining and their hoofs oiled. Mr. and Mrs. Lorimer, with Ben and Jamie, were bringing a picnic but only staying until around two because Mrs. Lorimer was taking Jamie to a party. Thalia's narg was going to a motorbike rally, so she would not be there at all.

Tarquin walked out with long, reaching strides, Thalia's heels niggling his sides to keep him in front of Willow. When they reached the road, Thalia let Tarquin trot on, his hoofs ringing on the road. Willow battered behind him, tossing her head, almost cantering to keep up.

"Here! Wait for us!" Sally shouted. "Willow's nearly sweating."

Thalia steadied Tarquin to a jog-trot.

"The show jumping starts at eleven, and our

class is first. If we don't keep going, we'll be late," she called back over her shoulder.

"They'll be worn out if you keep on at this rate," Sally muttered. But Thalia paid no attention to her.

They had been riding for almost half an hour when Tarquin went lame. Sally noticed it first, hearing the difference in his hoofbeats.

"You're crazy," snapped Thalia. "Tarquin's never lame."

But he was. In a few minutes even Thalia had to admit it. She stopped Tarquin and jumped to the ground.

"Near fore," said Sally, sliding down from Willow.

Thalia glared at Sally, but this time she didn't argue. She picked up Tarquin's foot. There was a small stone wedged between his shoe and the sole of his foot.

"Hoof pick, nurse," said Thalia, being a television doctor, but Sally did not have a hoof pick. They tried knocking the stone with a bigger one from the side of the road and working on it with a branch, but it remained firmly wedged under the rim of Tarquin's shoe.

A car passed and Thalia waved her arms wildly, shouting for help. It sped past, ignoring them.

"Putrid parsnips," Thalia yelled after it. "Holes in all your tires!"

Four more cars drove past before a rusty, tea-cozy car shuddered to a halt. A square woman in a tweed hat got out and asked what was wrong.

"It's a stone," explained Thalia. "Stuck in his shoe and we can't get it out."

"What you need is a Boy Scout," said the square woman, braying with laughter at her own wit.

"We're on our way to the Tarent show," said Thalia urgently. "I'm going to be late for the show jumping. You must have something in your car that would hook it out."

"Something in your picnic basket," suggested Sally, seeing a wicker basket on the backseat.

"Can opener!" exclaimed the woman. In seconds she had rustled out a solid, old-fashioned can opener, and while Thalia held up Tarquin's foot, she levered out the stone.

The stone came out so suddenly that the square woman staggered backward, almost sitting down on the road. Sally grabbed her arm to steady her. Thalia had already mounted and was trotting away, shouting her thanks.

"Couldn't wait," she cried when Sally caught up with her. "It's twenty past ten. We'll never make it in time for the jumping. It'll be over before we get there." She urged Tarquin into a canter.

Willow, trotting like a hackney horse, battered along behind him.

"You're going too fast. You shouldn't be cantering on the road," said Sally, but Thalia chose not to hear.

The board advertising Buxton's Free Range Eggs was painted red and white and couldn't be missed. It was definitely where they were to meet Simon, but there was no sign of him.

"Told you," shouted Thalia, pulling Tarquin to a jagged halt. "It's always a mess trying to meet someone. We're so late, I expect he got fed up waiting for us and went on."

"He wouldn't do that," said Sally, looking around anxiously for any sign of Simon.

Everything felt wrong to Sally—her stirrups uneven, her hard hat digging into the back of her neck, her stomach clenched into a solid, nervous lump—and it was all Thalia's fault for riding like an idiot.

"Well, he's not here, is he? Come on. We can't wait." As she spoke, Thalia rode Tarquin toward the road to the show.

"But I said we would wait."

"Not when we're so late! Oh, come on. Simon doesn't need us. Come on." Willow pawed the road, whinnying and fretting to follow Tarquin. For a moment Sally was tempted; then she remembered Clover.

"We must wait," she shouted. "If we're not here, Simon won't go to the show and they'll send Clover back to Miss Meek's."

"Well, I'm not waiting." Thalia eased her reins, letting Tarquin plunge forward.

Once the sound of Tarquin's hoofs had faded into silence, Willow stopped messing about and stood still, clinking her bit impatiently.

"Only a minute," Sally promised, patting Willow's sweaty shoulder. "Only a minute and he'll be here. Pretty rotten of Thalia. How would she like it if Simon had promised to meet her and then just ridden on?"

One minute turned into five minutes. Five minutes into ten. Horses and riders trotted past Sally, all smart and bright, all bound for the show. People looked down curiously from horse-trailer windows at Sally standing on the side of the road, holding Willow's reins.

At last Sally remounted.

"No use," she said to Willow. "He's not coming."

Then clear in her mind's eye she saw Clover standing in her narrow stall at the riding school, her tail matted, her eyes dead as she waited for another stranger to ride her up and down the lane. Sally shuddered, getting goose bumps.

"No!" she said aloud. "No!"

A young woman on a bay hunter pointed out which road would take her in the direction of the Moss. Sally urged Willow into a trot and rode away from the crossroads. She was going to find Simon. She was going to make him come to the show.

The road turned sharply to the left over a hump-backed bridge. There, sitting in a field gateway, was Simon, holding Clover's reins as she cropped the grass.

"Simon!" yelled Sally. "What's wrong? Why are you here? You were supposed to meet us at the crossroads. We're late. Really late. Come on."

Simon looked straight at Sally and she saw his face was white and strained, his eyes pink-rimmed.

"I'm not going to the show," he said. "I'm not riding."

Fervently Sally wished that Thalia was with her. She would have raged at Simon and made him ride. But there was only Sally. She took a deep breath.

"Don't you care?" she demanded, turning on Simon. "Don't you care about Clover? If you don't come to the show, your dad will send Clover back. Maybe it was your fault that your horse broke its leg. I don't know. But it *will* be your fault if Clover is sent back to the riding school. All you have to do is ride around the

Handy Horse and you've saved her. If you won't do that, you'll know it is your fault this time. Your fault if Clover is sent back. And when they've worked and worked for Miss Meek she sends them to the auctioneer, and you know what that means."

Simon sat without moving.

"Now. Come on, now!" ordered Sally.

Suddenly she remembered the unicorn lying secret in her jacket pocket. She took it out and it lay in her hand, its jewel-green eye glinting up at her. She leaned down to Simon.

"Hold out your hand," she said, and placed the unicorn on his palm. "It came out of the sea. You can keep it for today. It makes your wishes come true."

For a long minute Simon stared down at the brilliant, rainbowed unicorn. Then he closed his hand over it.

"Right," he said, looking up at Sally. "Okay."

He thrust the unicorn into his pocket and sprang to his feet.

"I'm doing this for you," he muttered to Clover, his hands shaking as he pulled up her girths. "Wouldn't want to be sent back to that riding school myself."

Twenty minutes later the Tarent Horse Show lay spread out in front of them. It was far bigger than Sally had ever imagined—billowing white tents, a patchwork of show rings, every size and shape of horse and pony, and a menagerie of beasts from haystack Highland cattle to miniature pigs.

No one paid any attention to Sally and Simon as they rode through the open gates and on past rows of stalls until they reached the juvenile show-jumping ring. A dark-skinned boy on a flashy chestnut was jumping in the ring.

As Sally steadied Willow to a halt, she felt her throat tighten, her mouth go suddenly dry. Worrying about Clover, she had almost forgotten that she was here to jump, and that she had never really jumped in public before. The red-and-white poles grew before her eyes into enormous jumps stretching skyward, filling the ring in strange patterns of doubles and triples.

Never, never could she jump those, Sally decided. They must be for a different class. There were far too high for Willow.

The boy rode out of the ring. A loudspeaker crackled, and a voice announced, "Last call for Sally Lorimer. Sally Lorimer, number sixty-nine, to ring four."

## *Chapter Nine*

The announcement broke over Sally like an icy wave.

"But I'm not ready," she said aloud. "Willow's not ready. We just got here." She stood up in her stirrups, searching for Thalia, thinking that Thalia could go and tell them that she wasn't jumping.

"There you are at last!" Mrs. Blair came striding toward her. "Where have you been? Never mind. Tell me later. Thalia took care of your entry, and I've got your number."

"I'm not . . ." began Sally, but Mrs. Blair was already tying number 69 around her arm.

"Nice little course. Jumps are numbered. Go around the outside, then across the center, over the double, back down over the wall, and that's it. Let's have another clear round for the jump-off."

"But Willow's never—"

"Go on, dear," said Mrs. Blair. She gripped Willow's bit-ring and marched them to the entrance. Then, with a pat on Willow's quarters, she sent them trotting into the ring.

For a second Sally had only one thought in her head—to get off Willow. Once she was on the ground, no one could make her jump.

"That's what you did before," said the voice in Sally's head. "You're not going to mess things up like that again, are you?"

And Sally knew she couldn't. She was here, and she had to jump.

A steward blew a whistle, and somehow Willow carried her through the start. With pricked ears, bright eyes, Willow cantered at the first jump.

Sally's reins were too long, fistfuls of leather that she couldn't sort out. Her feet were loose in her stirrups, and as Willow jumped, Sally collapsed onto her neck. There was the crash of falling poles behind them, and Willow was racing on to the next jump.

As they turned up the far side of the ring, Sally was completely out of control. She hardly knew where she was. The red-and-white poles seemed to rush at her. As Willow jumped, Sally hung on to her mane, waiting for the crash of poles falling behind them and the gasping, indrawn breath of the spectators.

At the top of the ring Sally hardly knew what to do next. She could only hear Mrs. Blair's voice filling her head, telling her that she had to cross the ring, jumping the double. She hauled Willow around, but at the first part of the double Willow swerved to one side and galloped past the jump.

Voices were shouting at Sally to stop. Someone was blowing a whistle. Sally caught a glimpse of Thalia's shocked face, Verity Blair standing beside her.

"Only the wall. I've got to jump it and then I've been around," Sally told herself. She tugged madly on one rein and turned Willow straight at the wall. In two bucking, galloping strides Willow was right under the wall. She rose straight into the air. For a second Sally seemed to hang in space—clear of the saddle, hands under her chin, clutching the buckle of her reins, one stirrup flying loose and her scream frozen in her throat. Clear over the wall, Sally crashed down onto the saddle and was carried out of the ring.

"Number sixty-nine, Sally Lorimer, is eliminated for taking the wrong course."

Sally tumbled to the ground, threw her arms around Willow's neck, and pressed her face against her mane. It was only now that Sally realized she had been crying. It had all been too sudden. She hadn't been ready, hadn't had time. The sound of crashing poles was still loud in her ears, her eyes still blurred by the brightness of the enormous jumps.

"Ladies and gentlemen, now that we have rebuilt the course, we have the jump-off for first place. Number sixty-eight, Thalia Nesbit, and number fifty-three, Verity Blair."

Sally blew her nose and scrubbed at her eyes. Looking straight ahead so that no one could see her, she found a place at ringside just in time to see Thalia win the toss and Verity ride in.

Buster cleared all the jumps from a solid canter, but he had two refusals. Tarquin pranced into the ring, mane and tail flying as he struggled against Thalia's control. Then with a half rear he was away, following an arching rainbow path around the whole course. Thalia's face was swallowed up in an excited grin.

"Clear round, number sixty-eight, Thalia Nesbit on Tarquin, our winner and, I think, our fastest round."

People clapped, ribbons were presented, and a short burst of marching music crashed out over the loudspeaker.

"Jealous?" Sally asked herself.

"No," she answered honestly. "Just wish I hadn't made such a mess of it, hadn't let Willow down."

"But you waited for Simon," consoled the voice. "Because you waited for him, it'll be okay for Clover. They'll keep her."

"Hi!" yelled Thalia, riding up with Verity, her whole being radiant with success.

"You were super. Tarquin just flew over them," said Sally, truly meaning it.

"Your horse jumped well," said Verity to Sally. "She jumped miles over the wall."

"We've got to give them our names at the tent," said Thalia, not mentioning Sally's performance. "Be back in a minute."

Sally stood watching them ride away together. "Verity should be Thalia's partner for the cross-country," she thought. "She'd be better than me."

Sally looked at her watch. It was nearly twelve. The pairs cross-country started at two. Two hours and she would be riding with Thalia over walls and barrels, drop jumps and banks. Sally shuddered and wrapped her arms tightly around herself as she watched other children riding up to Thalia and Verity to congratulate them.

She didn't want to wait for Thalia. Sally mounted Willow, turned her in the opposite direction, and began to ride slowly through the crowded life of the show. She leaned down over Willow's neck and fed her a peppermint.

"It was all my fault," she whispered. "You were the best horse."

Vaguely Sally was looking for the Handy Horse class. She hadn't seen Simon since they had ridden into the show. By now he would have ridden around the Handy Horse and Clover would be safe.

"If he hasn't run away," she thought.

"Sal! Sally!" called Ben, charging through the crowd toward Sally. "We've been looking for you for ages. We've got the picnic. Come on. Thalia's looking for you too. Hurry up. We can't stay long because of Jamie's party."

Sally rode beside her brother to where her family was sitting on the grass. A blanket was spread out on the ground and covered with picnic food. Her mother was filling rolls with cheese and lettuce. Her father was holding Meg and Misty.

Sally swallowed hard to clear the lump in her throat before she began to tell them about her disastrous round. But they knew already.

"Bad luck," said her father. "Thalia told us."

"At least you didn't fall off," said Ben.

Sally wanted to say *Wait for the cross-country,* but her voice wasn't there. She looked away, dragging her hand across her eyes.

"I've been looking for you everywhere," cried Thalia, pulling Tarquin to a halt just in time to stop him from plunging through the picnic. "We're supposed to have lunch with the Blairs. All the Pony Club people are there. They want you to come so they can get to know us."

Sally shook her head.

"Why not?" demanded Thalia impatiently. "It's good. They all like Willow."

"No."

"Forget it then," said Thalia, and galloped off.

"Is there a problem?" asked Mr. Lorimer. His wife gave him a quick look, warning him not to cause trouble.

Sitting close to Meg, Sally shared her food between dogs and horse. In spite of the sun she was cold. Cold and afraid. Afraid of the cross-country. If things went as wrong as they had that morning Willow could easily fall and break a leg.

"Are you sure you're feeling all right?" asked her mother. "If you're not feeling well, I'm sure we could find some way of getting Willow home to Kestrel Manor and you could come with us in the car."

"Of course not," said Sally. "I'm fine."

"Well," said her father, standing up. "We'll need to go if we're going to get Jamie to this party on time. Now, do be sensible. You don't have to ride in this cross-country thing if you don't feel like it."

"I'm fine," Sally repeated.

She watched them pack the picnic and go back to the car.

"Fine," she told herself again when her family had gone. "Fine, fine, fine. I'm Thalia's pair and I must ride around with her."

But Sally's head was filled with the sound of crashing poles. This afternoon the obstacles would be solid. They wouldn't knock down.

## *Chapter Ten*

"Don't tell me you're not ready! The junior cross-country's nearly finished, and then it's the pairs." Thalia's hard hat was under her arm, and her hair blazed around her head as she sat tall in the saddle. "We've still got to ride them."

Sally stared up at the silhouette of Thalia and Tarquin looming over her.

"Just tell her that you're not riding. Say you're not feeling well. Tell her your father is coming back for you," whispered the tempter in Sally's head.

She opened her mouth, ready to make excuses to Thalia, to say anything, anything, as long as she didn't have to ride over the cross-country.

"Do not be such a coward," said a voice that was deeper than Sally's mind. "Willow will take you around. Give in now and you'll hate yourself forever. Remember what it was like when you wouldn't gallop? Well?"

"Gosh," exclaimed Sally, struggling to her feet. "I didn't know it was that time." She mounted quickly and, gathering in her reins, patted Willow's shoulder.

"Right," she said to Thalia. "Where shall we go?"

"There's a bit of space over here," said Thalia, leading the way. "Why didn't you come and have lunch with us?"

Bumping behind Tarquin, Sally hardly heard a word Thalia was saying. She had forgotten everything she had ever known about riding, absolutely everything Martine had taught her.

Over to her left Sally could see the cross-country course laid out over the hillside—brush jumps, barrels, ditches, walls, and the sheen of a water jump. No one was jumping. Stewards were going around altering the obstacles. Sally supposed the junior class was over and they were getting the course ready for the pairs.

"If only I wasn't a pair," Sally thought desperately as she trotted and cantered Willow in a schooling circle. "Then it wouldn't matter.

Thalia could jump and it wouldn't matter what I did."

"Junior pairs cross-country," boomed the loudspeaker. "To the cross-country course now. This is class fifteen. About to begin—class fifteen."

"That's us," said Thalia. "We might as well go now." Willow followed Tarquin toward the start.

"What did you think of the stile?" Thalia called back over her shoulder. "They've never seen a stile before, and it's more or less straight into the water when they land."

"Stile?" echoed Sally, not knowing what Thalia was talking about.

Thalia looked back at Sally's blank face. "Don't tell me that you haven't walked the course?" she exclaimed, her voice light and false. "I was sure you'd have walked around with Ben."

It took Sally a minute to take in what Thalia had done—walked around the course without coming to tell her, walked around with the Blairs!

"Of all the stinking, disgusting things . . ."

Sally began, then bit back her words. Nothing she could say could possibly be bad enough. She glared furiously at Thalia.

"You know," she said, spitting out the words, "you know that I haven't seen the jumps, that I would never have thought of walking around the course. What a rotten thing to do. Just so you could be with the Blairs."

Through the throngs of horses, parents, and children gathered around the start, Sally caught sight of Simon trotting Clover toward them. In her fear of the cross-country Sally had completely forgotten about him. There was a blue ribbon on Clover's bridle, and Simon was beaming with success.

"You did it," cried Sally. "Oh, good! Good for Clover. Your father will have to keep her now."

"And I jumped. Measly two-inch pole, but I jumped it!"

"We're to go next," said Thalia. "I'll just have to tell you what jumps are next."

"Wait!" Simon took the unicorn out of his pocket and gave it back to Sally. "Magic," he said.

For a second Sally looked at it, rainbow in the palm of her hand, its golden horn glinting. She slipped it back into her pocket and rode Willow to the start.

Thalia held Tarquin on a tight rein. He was all energy, desperate to gallop and jump. Willow, too, pranced and pawed the ground, sensing Tarquin's excitement. Willow's ears were pricked and her eyes bright as she gazed out over the course, every bit as eager to gallop and jump as Tarquin.

"I'll count to three and then blow my whistle," said a wrinkled woman with straight white hair pulled back into a long ponytail.

Sally was still too furious even to look at Thalia. Her mind was filled with thoughts of Thalia's bossiness and nagging.

"Keep Willow up . . ." muttered Thalia.

"Don't you tell me what to do! Don't you dare. You wouldn't even wait for Simon. You went off with the Blairs—"

The whistle cut through Sally's fury, and instantly she rode Willow forward, plunging at Tarquin's side, urging Willow on.

The first jump, a stone wall, raced at Sally.

Nerves flickered in her stomach, but she was too mad at Thalia to notice.

Both horses soared over the wall, taking it in their stride like steeplechasers. They landed neck and neck. Sally never moved in the saddle. She jumped the wall as Thalia jumped, almost a part of her horse.

The course swung to the right. Rustic poles were in front of them and then behind.

"Brush next," shouted Thalia, but almost before she had spoken Sally felt Willow rise and reach out over the brush fence.

If the show jumping had been a blurred maze of jumps, the cross-country lay before Sally like a magic way, an enchanted path. Their galloping horses carried them winging high and clear over every obstacle.

"Next one's a drop," yelled Thalia. "Then downhill."

Sally glanced across at her, laughing for the joy and speed of their galloping. Thalia was grinning, laughing, caught in the same shared speed, the same delight.

Willow leaped out over the drop, and Sally felt the world fall away from her. They seemed to hang suspended in air before Willow's hoofs touched the ground again and they bucketed on downhill.

There was a jump of upended barrels and then a low turf bank, which both horses jumped—reaching heads, tucked-up knees—exactly side by side.

As they came to the stile Tarquin's gallop slowed to a canter, his eyes goggled. He snorted suspiciously through wide nostrils.

Out of the corner of her eye Sally saw him slowing down. He tried to swing to the side, but Thalia's legs, seat, and voice drove him on.

Suddenly Sally realized that she was in front. It was up to her to get Willow over the stile, and then Tarquin would follow.

"On you go," she whispered, sitting hard and neat in the saddle, riding her willing horse straight at the stile.

With a flick of her ears and swish of her tail Willow was over. As Sally trotted on into the wide stretch of water, she heard Tarquin land and come storming up behind her, showering her with spray.

Never again could Thalia taunt Sally for

being too slow. It was Willow who had given Tarquin a lead, Willow who had shown Tarquin the way.

They both cleared the in-and-out mini sheep pen. Then, leaping back over the first wall at a different place, they galloped through the finish together.

They slid from their horses, laughing and gasping.

"We were great!" exclaimed Thalia. "I knew we could do it. I kept telling you all you had to do was to keep up with Tarquin."

"And give him a lead!"

"He didn't stop. I kept him going. It wasn't a refusal."

"Clear round," Sally said triumphantly.

"I reckon," said Thalia.

They stood for a moment grinning at each other, not speaking.

"Listen," said Thalia, the words bursting out of her. "I didn't mean to be so rotten to you. Going on and on about Willow being slow. Honestly, I didn't mean to say some of the things I did. I just get all worked up and say things I don't mean afterward. I get so desperate for Tarquin to do well. It's a way of saying thank-you to Narg for being bothered with me. And I knew that if you would only wake Willow—" Thalia clapped her hand over her mouth.

"I won't say anything, ever again," Thalia mumbled through her fingers. "I'll buy a gag for myself and wear it always."

"That," said Sally, "would make you the most boring friend. And Tarquin would hate it if you couldn't talk to him! Anyway, you were right, even if you did go on a bit."

And in the excitement of the moment their days of quarreling were forgotten. For now Sally was as good a rider as Thalia, Willow as fast as Tarquin.

Simon's father came to shout his thanks to Sally for finding Clover.

"Boy's ready to ride again!" he roared. "Miracle! Miracle!"

"You will keep Clover?"

"Home with us until the day she dies. Give you my word."

Verity came to tell them that they were the

fastest pair. At last, when all the scores were in, they knew they had won. The only clear round out of eighteen entries.

The woman with the white ponytail presented their ribbons and a silver cup to be shared six months each. Mrs. Blair shook their hands and told them her heart had been in her mouth watching them going around. Sally pinched herself hard to make sure she wasn't dreaming.

"Now," said Mrs. Blair, looking at Thalia, "come over to my box. I want to have a word with you about our Pony Club team for the one-day event in November. I'm wondering if this year we might, just might . . ."

Thalia urged Tarquin forward at Mrs. Blair's side. Three fat women on Highland ponies, giggling together, rode in front of Sally. By the time they had ridden past, Thalia and Mrs. Blair were lost in the crowd. Sally, clutching the cup, was alone.

"It's because I made such a mess of the jumping this morning," Sally thought. "It's because they know I'm nervous."

She clenched her teeth and swallowed hard.

"Don't care," she thought. "I don't care if they don't want me."

She shivered, suddenly cold. No longer part of the bright day, no longer part of the milling life of the show.

"Sally!" Thalia pulled Tarquin to a rearing halt beside her. "What are you doing here? Didn't you hear Mrs. Blair?"

"That was you, not me."

"Oh, idiot! She wants you too," Thalia said, and stared at Sally, seeing her hurt disappointment. "I've told you I'm sorry for the things I said. And I am. Honest I am. I couldn't wait for Simon. It wasn't because I didn't care about him. I just had to get to the show jumping in time. I don't know why I walked around the course with the Blairs. I was coming to get you, honest. Then they shouted that there wasn't time, and . . . And I'm sorry you had to give Tarquin a lead over the stile because that makes Willow a better horse than him."

"Well, equal," said Sally, grinning.

"Willow more equal," said Thalia.

And they were both laughing.

"Okay?" said Thalia, and this time it was.

They rode home together, taking turns carrying the cup, Sally's ribbon safe in her pocket beside the unicorn.

When they had seen to their horses, they left them chomping pony nuts, oats, and bran.

"Dear Willow," murmured Sally, turning back for one last loving look at her horse—the flat cheekbones, the arch of her neck, the curve of her ears. "Thank you for everything." She swung away to chase after Thalia and run with her to Kestrel Manor.

They burst into the house together.

"We won the pairs!" shouted Thalia. "We were the best!"

"And Mrs. Blair wants us to be on the Pony Club team," cried Sally to her astonished family. "Both of us!"

Together Sally and Thalia raced through Kestrel Manor, Meg and Misty barking at their heels, Jamie running behind them as they stamped their way up the wide staircase.

"Pony Club team! Pony Club team!" they chanted. "Pony Club team!"

*Don't miss*

## *Pony Club Rider*

"Let's do some jumping," said Thalia.

"The field is pure mud," said Sally. She felt a cold clutch in her stomach as she remembered how badly she had been left behind when she had jumped on Saturday. "We'd only churn it up more."

"One turn each won't make any difference." Thalia was already turning Tarquin toward Kestrel Manor.

They rode across the horses' field to where the jumps were standing, abandoned for the winter.

"Hold his reins and I'll straighten them out a bit," said Thalia, jumping down from Tarquin.

Sally sat watching as Thalia struggled to set up four jumps in the muddy field. She did not want to jump. She felt cold and nervous, wanting to make up excuses about why she couldn't jump.

"Don't start that again," warned the voice in

her head. "You are on the Pony Club team now. Of course you want to jump."

"There," said Thalia. "How's that? Those four?"

Sally eyed the motley collection of poles, boxes, and oil drums that Thalia had set up. They seemed so high that no one in her right mind would think of jumping them.

She opened her mouth to say that she wasn't going to jump, that it was too muddy, that Willow might slip. Then she saw Thalia watching her with a fixed stare and heard herself saying, "I'll go first."

Tight and cold, Sally rode Willow in a circle and let her canter on at the first jump.

Willow pricked her ears and popped over the jump, timing it perfectly. Sally sat neat and still, going with her horse. She landed securely balanced, ready to ride on at the next jump. Her fear had vanished. Totally, completely, as if it had never been.

"For I can jump now," Sally thought. "Even if I do make mistakes and get mixed up, it doesn't matter—I can jump." She rode back to Thalia grinning broadly, because she knew now, and nothing could change it.